WITH INTENT TO STEAL

BY

ALGERNON BLACKWOOD

British Library Cataloguing-in-Publication Data
A catalogue record for this book is available from
the British Library

Contents

ALGERNON BLACKWOOD

Algernon Henry Blackwood was born in Shooter's Hill, South East England, in 1869. In his youth he trained as a doctor at Wellington College in Berkshire, and went on to pursue a number of careers, in areas as varied as milk farming, modelling, journalism and violin teaching. In his thirties, Blackwood returned to England from New York, where he had spent a number of years, and began to write stories of the supernatural.

Blackwood was extremely prolific, producing over the course of his life some ten original collections of short stories, fourteen novels, several children's books, and a number of plays. Most of his work was concerned with the ghostly, mythical or occult – themes which Blackwood was attracted to his whole life – and he is regarded as one of the earlier practitioners of 'weird fiction'. Amongst his best known short stories are 'The Wendigo', and 'The Willows' – a work which H. P. Lovecraft called "the finest weird story I have ever read." In 1914, he produced his short story collection *Incredible Adventures*, which leading literary critic

S. T. Joshi has said "may be the premier weird collection of this or any other century." Blackwood worked as an undercover agent for Britain during the First World War, and during the 1920s became famous for reading his ghost stories live on BBC radio and television.

After a number of strokes, Blackwood died in old age in Kent, England.

With Intent to Steal

Algernon Blackwood

To sleep in a lonely barn when the best bedrooms in the house were at our disposal, seemed, to say the least, unnecessary, and I felt that some explanation was due to our host.

But Shorthouse, I soon discovered, had seen to all that; our enterprise would be tolerated, not welcomed, for the master kept this sort of thing down with a firm hand. And then, how little I could get this man, Shorthouse, to tell me. There was much I wanted to ask and hear, but he surrounded himself with impossible barriers. It was ludicrous; he was surely asking a good deal of me, and yet he would give so little in return, and his reason – that it was for my good – may have been perfectly true, but did not bring me any comfort in its train. He gave me sops now and then, however, to keep up my curiosity, till I soon was aware that there were growing up side by side within me a genuine interest and an equally genuine fear; and something of both these is probably necessary to all real excitement.

The barn in question was some distance from the house, on the side of the stables, and I had passed it on several of my journeyings to and fro wondering at its forlorn and untarred appearance under a regime where everything was so spick and span; but it had never once occurred to me as possible that I should come to spend a night under its roof with a comparative stranger, and undergo there an experience belonging to an order of things I had always rather ridiculed and despised.

At the moment I can only partially recall the process by which Shorthouse persuaded me to lend him my company. Like myself, he was a guest in this autumn house-party, and where there were so many to chatter and to chaff, I think his taciturnity of manner had appealed to me by contrast, and that I wished to repay something of what I owed. There was, no doubt, flattery in it as well, for he was more than twice my age, a man of amazingly wide experience, an explorer of all the world's corners where danger lurked, and – most subtle flattery of all – by far the best shot in the whole party, our host included.

At first, however, I held out a bit.

3

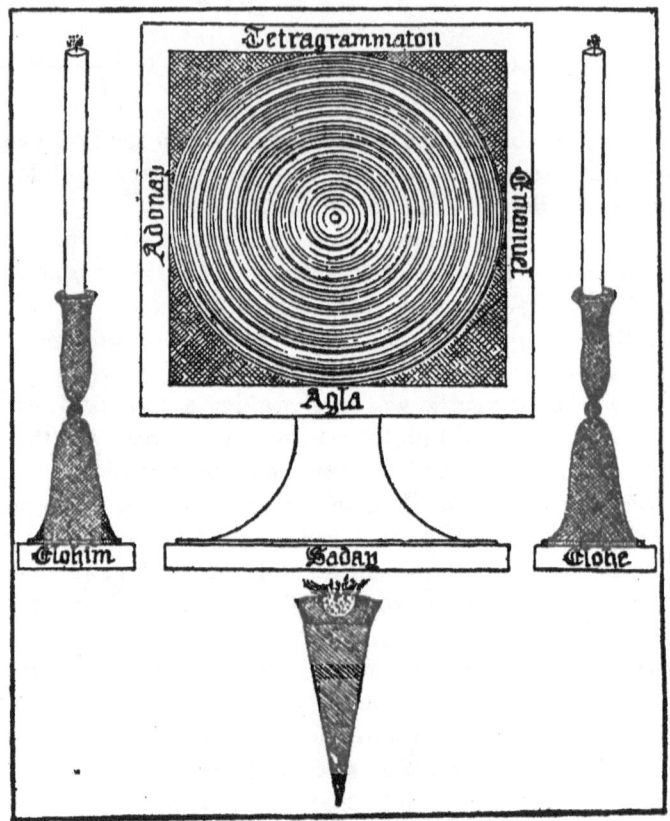

THE IMPLEMENTS OF MAGIC

'But surely this story you tell,' I said, 'has the parentage common to all such tales – a superstitious heart and an imaginative brain – and has grown now by frequent repetition into an authentic ghost story? Besides, this head gardener of half a century ago,' I added, seeing that he still went on cleaning his gun in silence, 'who was he, and what positive information have you about him beyond the fact that he was found hanging from the rafters, dead?'

'He was no mere head gardener, this man who passed as such,' he replied without looking up, 'but a fellow of splendid education who used this curious disguise for his own purposes. Part of this

very barn, of which he always kept the key, was found to have been
fitted up as a complete laboratory, with athanor, alembic, cucurbite,
and other appliances, some of which the master destroyed at once
– perhaps for the best – and which I have only been able to guess
at – '

'Black arts,' I laughed.

'Who knows?' he rejoined quietly. 'The man undoubtedly possessed knowledge – dark knowledge – that was most unusual and
dangerous, and I can discover no means by which he came to it –
no ordinary means, that is. But I *have* found many facts in the case
which point to the exercise of a most desperate and unscrupulous
will; and the strange disappearances in the neighbourhood, as well
as the bones found buried in the kitchen garden, though never
actually traced to him, seem to me full of dreadful suggestion.'

I laughed again, a little uncomfortably perhaps, and said it
reminded one of the story of Gilles de Rais, *maréchal* of France, who
was said to have killed and tortured to death in a few years no
less than one hundred and sixty women and children for the purposes of necromancy, and who was executed for his crimes at
Nantes. But Shorthouse would not 'rise', and only returned to his
subject.

'His suicide seems to have been only just in time to escape
arrest,' he said.

'A magician of no high order then,' I observed sceptically, 'if
suicide was his only way of evading the country police.'

'The police of London and St Petersburg r⬛⬛⬛r, returned
Shorthouse; 'for the headquarters of this pretty company was somewhere in Russia, and his apparatus all bore the marks of the most
skilful foreign make. A Russian woman then employed in the house-
hold – governess, or something – vanished, too, about the same time
and was never caught. She was no doubt the cleverest of the lot.
And, remember, the object of this appalling group was not mere
vulgar gain, but a kind of knowledge that called for the highest
qualities of courage and intellect in the seekers.'

I admit I was impressed by the man's conviction of voice and
manner, for there is something very compelling in the force of an
earnest man's belief, though I still affected to sneer politely.

'But, like most black magicians, the fellow only succeeded in
compassing his own destruction – that of his tools, rather, and of
escaping himself.'

'So that he might better accomplish his objects *elsewhere and otherwise*,' said Shorthouse, giving, as he spoke, the most minute attention to the cleaning of the lock.

'Elsewhere and otherwise,' I gasped.

'As if the shell he left hanging from the rafter in the barn in no way impeded the man's spirit from continuing his dreadful work under new conditions,' he added quietly, without noticing my interruption. 'The idea being that he sometimes revisits the garden and the barn, chiefly the barn – '

'The barn!' I exclaimed; 'for what purpose?'

'Chiefly the barn,' he finished, as if he had not heard me, 'that is, when there is anybody in it.'

I stared at him without speaking, for there was a wonder in me how he would add to this.

'When he wants fresh material, that is – he comes to steal from the living.'

'Fresh material!' I repeated aghast. 'To steal from the living!' Even then, in broad daylight, I was foolishly conscious of a creeping sensation at the roots of my hair, as if a cold breeze were passing over my skull.

'The strong vitality of the living is what this sort of creature is supposed to need most,' he went on imperturbably, 'and where he has worked and thought and struggled before is the easiest place for him to get it in. The former conditions are in some way more easily reconstructed – ' He stopped suddenly, and devoted all his attention to the gun. 'It's difficult to explain, you know, rather,' he added presently, 'and, besides, it's much better that you should not know till afterwards.'

I made a noise that was the beginning of a score of questions and of as many sentences, but it got no further than a mere noise, and Shorthouse, of course, stepped in again.

'Your scepticism,' he added, 'is one of the qualities that induce me to ask you to spend the night there with me.

'In those days,' he went on, in response to my urging for more information, 'the family were much abroad, and often travelled for years at a time. This man was invaluable in their absence. His wonderful knowledge of horticulture kept the gardens – French, Italian, English – in perfect order. He had *carte blanche* in the matter of expense, and of course selected all his own underlings. It was the sudden, unexpected return of the master that surprised the amazing stories of the countryside before the fellow, with all his cleverness, had time to prepare or conceal.'

'But is there no evidence, no more recent evidence, to show that something is likely to happen if we sit up there?' I asked, pressing him yet further, and I think to his liking, for it showed at least that I was interested. 'Has anything happened there lately, for instance?'

Shorthouse glanced up from the gun he was cleaning so asiduously, and the smoke from his pipe curled up into an odd twist between me and the black beard and oriental, sun-tanned face. The magnetism of his look and expression brought more sense of conviction to me than I had felt hitherto, and I realised that there had been a sudden little change in my attitude and that I was now much more inclined to go in for the adventure with him. At least, I thought, with such a man, one would be safe in any emergency; for he is determined, resourceful, and to be depended upon.

'There's the point,' he answered slowly; 'for there has apparently been a fresh outburst – an attack almost, it seems – quite recently. There is evidence, of course, plenty of it, or I should not feel the interest I do feel, but – ' he hesitated a moment, as though considering how much he ought to let me know, 'but the fact is that three men this summer, on separate occasions, who have gone into that barn after nightfall, have been *accosted* – '

'Accosted?' I repeated, betrayed into the interruption by his choice of so singular a word.

'And one of the stablemen – a recent arrival and quite ignorant of the story – who had to go in there late one night, saw a dark substance hanging down from one of the rafters, and when he climbed up, shaking all over, to cut it down – for he said he felt sure it was a corpse – the knife passed through nothing but air, and he heard a sound up under the eaves as if someone were laughing. Yet, while he slashed away, and afterwards too, the thing went on swinging there before his eyes and turning slowly with its own weight, like a huge joint on a spit. The man declares, too, that it had a large bearded face, and that the mouth was open and drawn down like the mouth of a hanged man.'

'Can we question this fellow?'

'He's gone – gave notice at once, but not before I had questioned him myself very closely.'

'Then this was quite recent?' I said, for I knew Shorthouse had not been in the house more than a week.

'Four days ago,' he replied. 'But, more than that, only three days ago a couple of men were in there together in full daylight when one of them suddenly turned deadly faint. He said that he felt an overmastering impulse to hang himself : and he looked about for a rope and was furious when his companion tried to prevent him – '

'But he did prevent him?'

'Just in time, but not before he had clambered on to a beam. He was very violent.'

I had so much to say and ask that I could get nothing out in time, and Shorthouse went on again.

'I've had a sort of watching brief for this case,' he said with a smile, whose real significance, however, completely escaped me at the time, 'and one of the most disagreeable features about it is the deliberate way the servants have invented excuses to go out to the place, and always after dark; some of them who have no right to go there, and no real occasion at all – have never been there in their lives before probably – and now all of a sudden have shown the keenest desire and determination to go out there about dusk, or soon after, and with the most paltry and foolish excuses in the world. Of course,' he added, 'they have been prevented, but the desire, stronger than their superstitious dread, and which they cannot explain, is very curious.'

'Very,' I admitted, feeling that my hair was beginning to stand up again.

'You see,' he went on presently, 'it all points to volition – in fact to deliberate arrangement. It is no mere family ghost that goes with every ivied house in England of a certain age; it is something real, and something very malignant.'

He raised his face from the gun barrel, and for the first time his eye caught mine in the full. Yes, he was very much in earnest. Also, he knew a great deal more than he meant to tell.

'It's worth tempting – and fighting, *I* think,' he said; 'but I want a companion with me. Are you game?' His enthusiasm undoubtedly caught me, but I still wanted to hedge a bit.

'I'm very sceptical,' I pleaded.

'All the better,' he said, almost as if to himself. 'You have the pluck; I have the knowledge – '

'The knowledge?'

He looked round cautiously as if to make sure that there was no one within earshot.

'I've been in the place myself,' he said in a lowered voice, 'quite lately – in fact only three nights ago – the day the man turned queer.'

I stared.

'But – I was obliged to come out –'

Still I stared.

'Quickly,' he added significantly.

'You've gone into the thing pretty thoroughly,' was all I could find to say, for I had almost made up my mind to go with him, and was not sure that I wanted to hear too much beforehand.

He nodded. 'It's a bore, of course, but I must do everything thoroughly – or not at all.'

'That's why you clean your own gun, I suppose?'

'That's why, when there's any danger, I take as few chances as possible,' he said, with the same enigmatical smile I had noticed before; and then he added with emphasis, 'And that is also why I ask you to keep me company now.'

Of course, the shaft went straight home, and I gave my promise without further ado.

Our preparations for the night – a couple of rugs and a flask of black coffee – were not elaborate, and we found no difficulty, about ten o'clock, in absenting ourselves from the billiard-room without attracting curiosity. Shorthouse met me by arrangement under the cedar on the back lawn, and I at once realised with vividness what a difference there is between making plans in the daytime and carrying them out in the dark. One's common sense – at least in matters of this sort – is reduced to a minimum, and imagination with all her attendant sprites usurps the place of judgment. Two and two no longer make four – they make a mystery, and the mystery loses no time in growing into a menace. In this particular case, however, my imagination did not find wings very readily, for I knew that my companion was the most *unmovable* of men – an unemotional, solid block of a man who would never lose his head, and in any conceivable state of affairs would always take the right as well as the strong course. So my faith in the man gave me a false courage that was nevertheless very consoling, and I looked forward to the night's adventure with a genuine appetite.

Side by side, and in silence, we followed the path that skirted the East Woods, as they were called, and then led across two hay fields, and through another wood, to the barn, which thus lay about half a mile from the Lower Farm. To the Lower Farm, indeed, it properly belonged; and this made us realise more clearly how very ingenious must have been the excuses of the Hall servants who felt the desire to visit it.

It had been raining during the late afternoon, and the trees were still dripping heavily on all sides, but the moment we left the second wood and came out into the open, we saw a clearing with the stars overhead, against which the barn outlined itself in a black, lugubrious shadow. Shorthouse led the way – still without a word – and we crawled in through a low door and seated ourselves in a soft heap of hay in the extreme corner.

'Now,' he said, speaking for the first time, 'I'll show you the inside of the barn, so that you may know where you are, and what to do, in case anything happens.'

A match flared in the darkness, and with the help of two more that followed I saw the interior of a lofty and somewhat rickety-looking barn, erected upon a wall of grey stones that ran all round and extended to a height of perhaps four feet. Above this masonry rose the wooden sides, running up into the usual vaulted roof, and supported by a double tier of massive oak rafters, which stretched across from wall to wall and were intersected by occasional uprights. I felt as if we were inside the skeleton of some antediluvian monster whose huge black ribs completely enfolded us. Most of this, of course, only sketched itself to my eye in the uncertain light of the flickering matches, and when I said I had seen enough, and the matches went out, we were at once enveloped in an atmosphere as densely black as anything that I have ever known. And the silence equalled the darkness.

We made ourselves comfortable and talked in low voices. The rugs, which were very large, covered our legs; and our shoulders sank into a really luxurious bed of softness. Yet neither of us apparently felt sleepy. I certainly didn't, and Shorthouse, dropping his customary brevity that fell little short of gruffness, plunged into an easy run of talking that took the form after a time of personal reminiscences. This rapidly became a vivid narration of adventure and travel in far countries, and at any other time I should have allowed myself to become completely absorbed in what he told. But, unfortunately, I was never able for a single instant to forget the real purpose of our enterprise, and consequently I felt all my senses more keenly on the alert than usual, and my attention accordingly more or less distracted. It was, indeed, a revelation to hear Shorthouse unbosom himself in this fashion, and to a young man it was of course doubly fascinating; but the little sounds that always punctuate even the deepest silence out of doors claimed some portion of my attention, and as the night grew on I soon became aware that his tales seemed somewhat disconnected and abrupt – and that, in fact, I heard really only part of them.

It was not so much that I actually heard other sounds, but that I *expected* to hear them; this was what stole the other half of my listening. There was neither wind nor rain to break the stillness, and certainly there were no physical presences in our neighbourhood, for we were half a mile even from the Lower Farm; and from the Hall and stables, at least a mile. Yet the stillness was being continually broken – perhaps *disturbed* is a better word – and it was to these very remote and tiny disturbances that I felt compelled to devote at least half my listening faculties.

From time to time, however, I made a remark or asked a question, to show that I was listening and interested; but, in a sense, my questions always seemed to bear in one direction and to make for one issue, namely, my companion's previous experience in the barn when he had been obliged to come out 'quickly'.

Apparently I could not help myself in the matter, for this was really the one consuming curiosity I had; and the fact that it was better for me not to know it made me the keener to know it all, even the worst.

Shorthouse realised this even better than I did. I could tell it by the way he dodged, or wholly ignored, my questions, and this subtle sympathy between us showed plainly enough, had I been able at the time to reflect upon its meaning, that the nerves of both of us were in a very sensitive and highly-strung condition. Probably, the complete confidence I felt in his ability to face whatever might happen, and the extent to which also I relied upon him for my own courage, prevented the exercise of my ordinary powers of reflection, while it left my senses free to a more than usual degree of activity.

Things must have gone on in this way for a good hour or more, when I made the sudden discovery that there was something unusual in the conditions of our environment. This sounds a roundabout mode of expression, but I really know not how else to put it. The discovery almost rushed upon me. By rights, we were two men waiting in an alleged haunted barn for something to happen; and.

as two men who trusted one another implicitly (though for very different reasons) there should have been two minds keenly alert, with the ordinary senses in active co-operation. Some slight degree of nervousness, too, there might also have been, but beyond this, nothing. It was therefore with something of dismay that I made the sudden discovery that there *was* something more, and something that I ought to have noticed very much sooner than I actually did notice it.

The fact was – Shorthouse's stream of talk was wholly unnatural. He was talking with a purpose. He did not wish to be cornered by my questions, true, but he had another and a deeper purpose still, and it grew upon me, as an unpleasant deduction from my discovery, that this strong, cynical, unemotional man by my side was talking – and had been talking all this time – to gain a particular end. And this end, I soon felt clearly, was to *convince himself*. But, of what?

For myself, as the hours wore on towards midnight, I was not anxious to find the answer; but in the end it became impossible to avoid it, and I knew as I listened, that he was pouring forth this steady stream of vivid reminiscences of travel – South Seas, big game, Russian exploration, women, adventures of all sorts – *because he wished the past to reassert itself to the complete exclusion of the present.* He was taking his precautions. He was afraid.

I felt a hundred things, once this was clear to me, but none of them more than the wish to get up at once and leave the barn. If Shorthouse was afraid already, what in the world was to happen to me in the long hours that lay ahead? . . . I only know that, in my fierce efforts to deny to myself the evidence of his partial collapse, the strength came that enabled me to play my part properly, and I even found myself helping him by means of animated remarks upon his stories, and by more or less judicious questions. I also helped him by dismissing from my mind any desire to enquire into the truth of his former experience; and it was good I did so, for had he turned it loose on me, with those great powers of convincing description that he had at his command, I verily believe that I should never have crawled from that barn alive. So, at least, I felt at the moment. It was the instinct of self-preservation, and it brought sound judgment.

Here, then, at least, with different motives, reached, too, by opposite ways, we were both agreed upon one thing, namely, that

The famous photograph of Sir Arthur Conan Doyle in which a 'spirit figure' appears.

Gerald Gardner conducting an occult ceremonial.

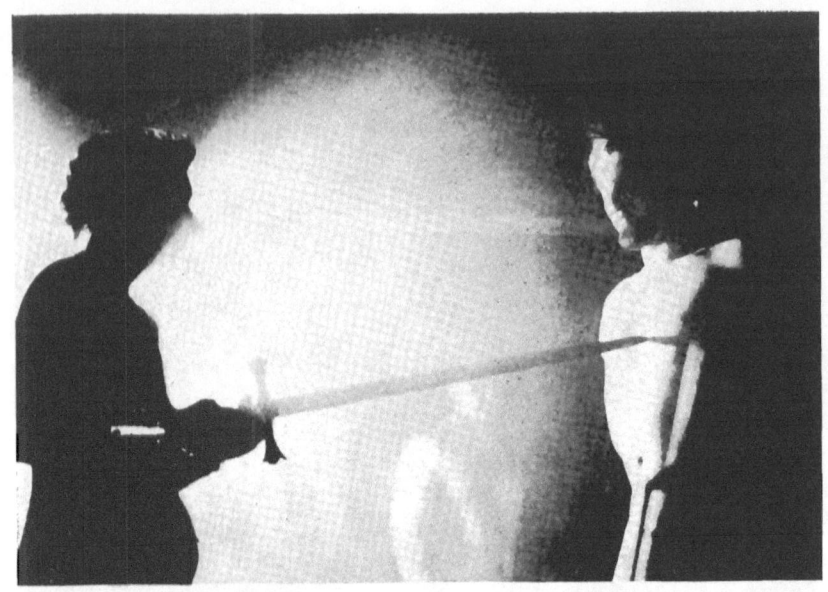

A priestess of *Wica* initiates a new member to her coven.

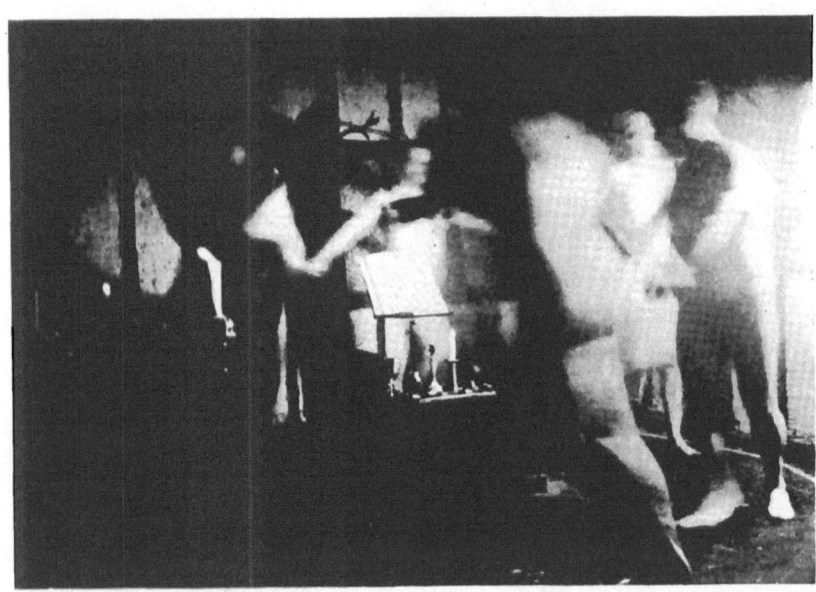

A present-day coven of witches celebrating their ancient rites.

temporarily we would forget. Fools we were, for a dominant emotion is not so easily banished, and we were for ever recurring to it in a hundred ways direct and indirect. A real fear cannot be so easily trifled with, and while we toyed on the surface with thousands and thousands of words – mere words – our sub-conscious activities were steadily gaining force, and would before very long have to be properly acknowledged. We could not get away from it. At last, when he had finished the recital of an adventure which brought him near enough to a horrible death, I admitted that in my uneventful life I had never yet been face to face with a real fear. It slipped out inadvertently, and, of course, without intention, but the tendency in him at the time was too strong to be resisted. He saw the loophole, and made for it full tilt.

'It is the same with all the emotions,' he said. 'The experiences of others never give a complete account. Until a man has deliberately turned and faced for himself the fiends that chase him down the years, he has no knowledge of what they really are, or of what they can do. Imaginative authors may write, moralists may preach, and scholars may criticise, but they are dealing all the time in a coinage of which they know not the actual value. Their listener gets a sensation – but not the true one. Until you have faced these emotions,' he went on, with the same race of words that had come from him the whole evening, 'and made them your own, your slaves, you have no idea of the power that is in them – hunger, that shows lights beckoning beyond the grave; thirst, that fills with mingled ice and fire; passion, love, loneliness, revenge, and –' he paused for a minute, and though I knew we were on the brink I was powerless to hold him. '. . . And fear,' he went on – 'fear . . . I think that death from fear, or madness from fear, must sum up in a second of time the total of all the most awful sensations it is possible for a man to know.'

'Then you have yourself felt something of this fear,' I interrupted; 'for you said just now –'

'I do not mean physical fear,' he replied; 'for that is more or less a question of nerves and will, and it is imagination that makes men cowards. I mean an *absolute* fear, a physical fear one might call it, that reaches the soul and withers every power one possesses.'

He said a lot more, for he, too, was wholly unable to stem the torrent once it broke loose; but I have forgotten it; or, rather,

G

mercifully I did not hear it, for I stopped my ears and only heard the occasional words when I took my fingers out to find if he had come to an end. In due course he did come to an end, and there we left it, for I then knew positively what he already knew : that somewhere here in the night, and within the walls of this very barn where we were sitting, there was waiting Something of dreadful malignancy and of great power, Something that we might both have to face ere morning, and Something that he had already tried to face once and failed in the attempt.

The night wore slowly on; and it gradually became more and more clear to me that I could not dare to rely as at first upon my companion, and that our positions were undergoing a slow process of reversal. I thank Heaven this was not borne in upon me too suddenly; and that I had at least the time to readjust myself somewhat to the new conditions. Preparation was possible, even if it was not much, and I sought by every means in my power to gather up all the shreds of my courage, so that they might together make a decent rope that would stand the strain when it came. The strain would come, that was certain, and I was thoroughly well aware – though for my life I cannot put into words the reasons for my knowledge – that the massing of the material against us was proceeding somewhere in the darkness with determination and a horrible skill besides.

Shorthouse meanwhile talked without ceasing. The great quantity of hay opposite – or straw, I believe it actually was – seemed to deaden the sound of his voice, but the silence, too, had become so oppressive that I welcomed his torrrent and even dreaded the moment when it would stop. I heard, too, the gentle ticking of my watch. Each second uttered its voice and dropped away into a gulf, as if starting on a journey whence there was no return. Once a dog barked somewhere in the distance, probably on the Lower Farm; and once an owl hooted close outside and I could hear the swishing of its wings as it passed overhead. Above me, in the darkness, I could just make out the outline of the barn, sinister and black, the rows of rafters stretching across from wall to wall like wicked arms that pressed upon the hay. Shorthouse, deep in some involved yarn of the South Seas that was meant to be full of cheer and sunshine, and yet only succeeded in making a ghastly mixture of unnatural colouring, seemed to care little whether I listened or not. He made no appeal to me, and I made one or two quite irrelevant remarks which passed him by and proved that he was merely uttering sounds. He, too, was afraid of the silence.

I fell to wondering how long a man could talk without stopping. . . . Then it seemed to me that these words of his went falling into the same gulf where the seconds dropped, only they were heavier and fell faster. I began to chase them. Presently one of them fell much faster than the rest, and I pursued it and found myself almost immediately in a land of clouds and shadows. They rose up and enveloped me, pressing on the eyelids. . . . It must have been just here that I actually fell asleep, somewhere between twelve and one o'clock, because, as I chased this word at tremendous speed through space, I knew that I had left the other words far, very far behind me, till, at last, I could no longer hear them at all. The voice of the story-teller was beyond the reach of hearing; and I was falling with ever increasing rapidity through an immense void.

A sound of whispering roused me. Two persons were talking under their breath close beside me. The words in the main escaped me, but I caught every now and then bitten-off phrases and half sentences, to which, however, I could attach no intelligible meaning. The words were quite close – at my very side in fact – and one of the voices sounded so familiar, that curiosity overcame dread, and I turned to look. I was not mistaken; *it was Shorthouse whispering*. But the other person, who must have been just a little beyond him, was lost in the darkness and invisible to me. It seemed then that Shorthouse at once turned up his face and looked at me and, by some means or other that caused me no surprise at the time, I easily made out the features in the darkness. They wore an expression I had never seen there before; he seemed distressed, exhausted, worn out, and as though he were about to give in after a long mental struggle. He looked at me, almost beseechingly, and the whispering of the other person died away.

'They're at me,' he said.

I found it quite impossible to answer; the words stuck in my throat. His voice was thin, plaintive, almost like a child's.

'I shall have to go. I'm not as strong as I thought. They'll call it suicide, but, of course, it's really murder.' There was real anguish in his voice and it terrified me.

A deep silence followed these extraordinary words, and I somehow understood that the Other Person was just going to carry on the conversation – I even fancied I saw lips shaping themselves just over my friend's shoulder -- when I felt a sharp blow in the ribs and a voice, this time a deep voice, sounded in my ear. I opened my eyes, and the wretched dream vanished. Yet it left behind it an impression of a strong and quite unusual reality.

'*Do* try not to go to sleep again,' he said sternly. 'You seem exhausted. Do you feel so?' There was a note in his voice I did not welcome -- less than alarm, but certainly more than mere solicitude.

'I do feel terribly sleepy all of a sudden,' I admitted, ashamed.

'So you may,' he added very earnestly; 'but I rely on you to keep awake, if only to watch. You have been asleep for half an hour at least -- and you were so still -- I thought I'd wake you --'

'Why?' I asked, for my curiosity and nervousness were altogether too strong to be resisted. 'Do you think we are in danger?'

'I think *they* are about here now. I feel my vitality going rapidly -- that's always the first sign. You'll last longer than I, remember. Watch carefully.'

The conversation dropped. I was afraid to say all I wanted to say. It would have been too unmistakably a confession; and intuitively I realised the danger of admitting the existence of certain emotions until positively forced to. But presently Shorthouse began again. His voice sounded odd, and as if it had lost power. It was more like a woman's or a boy's voice than a man's, and recalled the voice in my dream.

'I suppose you've got a knife?' he asked.

'Yes -- a big clasp knife; but why?' He made no answer. 'You don't think a practical joke likely? No one suspects we're here,' I went on. Nothing was more significant of our real feelings this night than the way we toyed with words, and never dared more than to skirt the things in our mind.

'It's just as well to be prepared,' he answered evasively. 'Better be quite sure. See which pocket it's in -- so as to be ready.'

I obeyed mechanically, and told him. But even this scrap of talk proved to me that he was getting further from me all the time in his mind. He was following a line that was strange to me, and, as he distanced me, I felt that the sympathy between us grew more and more strained. *He knew more*; it was not that I minded so much -- but that he was willing to *communicate less*. And in proportion as I lost his support, I dreaded his increasing silence. Not of words -- for he talked more volubly than ever, and with a fiercer purpose – but his silence in giving no hint of what he must have known to be really going on the whole time.

The night was perfectly still. Shorthouse continued steadily talking, and I jogged him now and again with remarks or questions in order to keep awake. He paid no attention, however, to either.

About two in the morning a short shower fell, and the drops rattled sharply on the roof like shot. I was glad when it stopped, for it completely drowned all other sounds and made it impossible to hear anything else that might be going on. Something *was* going on, too, all the time, though for the life of me I could not say what. The outer world had grown quite dim – the house-party, the shooters, the billiard-room, and the ordinary daily incidents of my visit. All my energies were concentrated on the present, and the constant strain of watching, waiting, listening, was excessively telling.

Shorthouse still talked of his adventures, in some Eastern country now, and less connectedly. These adventures, real or imaginary, had quite a savour of the Arabian Nights, and did not by any means make it easier for me to keep my hold on reality. The lightest weight will affect the balance under such circumstances, and in this case the weight of his talk was on the wrong scale. His words were very rapid, and I found it overwhelmingly difficult not to follow them into that great gulf of darkness where they all rushed and vanished. But that, I knew, meant sleep again. Yet, it was strange I should feel sleepy when at the same time all my nerves were fairly tingling. Every time I heard what seemed like a step outside, or a movement in the hay opposite, the blood stood still for a moment in my veins. Doubtless, the unremitting strain told upon me more than I realised, and this was doubly great now that I knew Shorthouse was a source of weakness instead of strength, as I had counted. Certainly, a curious sense of languor grew upon me more and more, and I was sure that the man beside me was engaged in the same struggle. The feverishness of his talk proved this, if nothing else. It was dreadfully hard to keep awake.

But this time, instead of dropping into the gulf, I saw something come up out of it! It reached our world by a door in the side of the barn furthest from me, and it came in cautiously and silently and moved into the mass of hay opposite. There, for a moment, I lost it, but presently I caught it again higher up. It was clinging, like a great bat, to the side of the barn. Something trailed behind it, I could not make out what. . . . It crawled up the wooden wall and began to move out along one of the rafters. A numb terror settled down all over me as I watched it. The thing trailing behind it was apparently a rope.

The whispering began again just then, but the only words I could catch seemed without meaning; it was almost like another language. The voices were above me, under the roof. Suddenly I saw signs of active movement going on just beyond the place where the thing lay upon the rafter. There was something else up there with it! Then followed panting, like the quick breathing that accompanies effort, and the next minute a black mass dropped through the air and dangled at the end of the rope.

Instantly, it all flashed upon me. I sprang to my feet and rushed headlong across the floor of the barn. How I moved so quickly in the darkness I do not know; but, even as I ran, it flashed into my mind that I should never get at my knife in time to cut the thing down, or else that I should find it had been taken from me. Somehow or other – the Goddess of Dreams knows how – I climbed up by the hay bales and swung out along the rafter. I was hanging, of course, by my arms, and the knife was already between my teeth, though I had no recollection of how it got there. It was open. The mass, hanging like a side of bacon, was only a few feet in front of me, and I could plainly see the dark line of rope that fastened it to the beam. I then noticed for the first time that it was swinging and turning in the air, and that as I approached it seemed to move along the beam, so that the same distance was always maintained between us. The only thing I could do – for there was no time to hesitate – was to jump at it through the air and slash at the rope as I dropped.

I seized the knife with my right hand, gave a great swing of my body with my legs and leaped forward at it through the air. Horrors! It was closer to me than I knew, and I plunged full into it, and the arm with the knife missed the rope and cut deeply into some substance that was soft and yielding. But, as I dropped past it, the thing had time to turn half its width so that it swung round and faced me – and I could have sworn as I rushed past it through the air, that it had the features of Shorthouse.

The shock of this brought the vile nightmare to an abrupt end, and I woke up a second time on the soft hay-bed to find that the grey dawn was stealing in, and that I was exceedingly cold. After all I had failed to keep awake, and my sleep, since it was growing light, must have lasted at least an hour. A whole hour off my guard!

There was no sound from Shorthouse, to whom, of course, my first thoughts turned; probably his flow of words had ceased long ago, and he too had yielded to the persuasions of the seductive god. I turned to wake him and get the comfort of companionship for the horror of my dream, when to my utter dismay I saw that the place where he had been was vacant. He was no longer beside me.

It had been no little shock before to discover that the ally in whom lay all my faith and dependence was really frightened, but it is quite impossible to describe the sensations I experienced when I realised he had gone altogether and that I was alone in the barn. For a minute or two my head swam and I felt a prey to a helpless terror. The dream, too, still seemed half real, so vivid had it been! I was thoroughly frightened – hot and cold by turns – and I clutched the hay at my side in handfuls, and for some moments had no idea in the world what I should do.

This time, at least, I was unmistakably awake, and I made a great effort to collect myself and face the meaning of the disappearance of my companion. In this I succeeded so far that I decided upon a thorough search of the barn, inside and outside. It was a dreadful undertaking, and I did not feel at all sure of being able to bring it to a conclusion, but I knew pretty well that unless something was done at once, I should simply collapse.

But, when I tried to move, I found that the cold, and fear, and I know not what else unholy besides, combined to make it almost impossible. I suddenly realised that a tour of inspection, during the whole of which my back would be open to attack, was not to be thought of. My will was not equal to it. Anything might spring upon me any moment from the dark corners, and the growing light was just enough to reveal every movement I made to any who might be watching. For, even then, and while I was still half dazed and stupid, I knew perfectly well that someone was watching me all the time with the utmost intentness. I had not merely awakened; I had *been* awakened.

I decided to try another plan; I called to him. My voice had a thin weak sound, far away and quite unreal, and there was no answer to it. Hark, though! There was something that might have been a very faint voice near me!

I called again, this time with greater distinctness, 'Shorthouse, where are you? Can you hear me?'

There certainly was a sound, but it was not a voice. Something was moving. It was someone shuffling along, and it seemed to be outside the barn. I was afraid to call again, and the sound continued. It was an ordinary sound enough, no doubt, but it came to me just then as something unusual and unpleasant. Ordinary sounds remain ordinary only so long as one is not listening to them; under the influence of intense listening they become unusual, portentous, and therefore extraordinary. So, this common sound came to me as something uncommon, disagreeable. It conveyed, too, an impression of stealth. And with it there was another, a slighter sound.

Just at this minute the wind bore faintly over the field the sound of the stable clock, a mile away. It was three o'clock; the hour when life's pulses beat lowest; when poor souls lying between life and death find it hardest to resist. Vividly I remember this thought crashing through my brain with a sound of thunder, and I realised that the strain on my nerves was nearing the limit, and that something would have to be done at once if I was to reclaim my self-control at all.

When thinking over afterwards the events of this dreadful night, it has always seemed strange to me that my second nightmare, so vivid in its terror and its nearness, should have furnished me with no inkling of what was really going on all this while; and that I should not have been able to put two and two together, or have discovered sooner than I did *what* this sound was and *where* it came from. I can well believe that the vile scheming which lay behind the whole experience found it an easy trifle to direct my hearing amiss; though, of course, it may equally well have been due to the confused condition of my mind at the time and to the general nervous tension under which I was undoubtedly suffering.

But, whatever the cause for my stupidity at first in failing to trace the sound to its proper source, I can only say here that it was with a shock of unexampled horror that my eye suddenly glanced upwards and caught sight of the figure moving in the shadows above my head among the rafters. Up to this moment I had thought that it was somebody outside the barn, crawling round the walls till it came to a door; and the rush of horror that froze my heart when I looked up and saw that it was Shorthouse creeping stealthily along a beam, is something altogether beyond the power of words to describe.

He was staring intently down upon me, and I knew at once that it was he who had been watching me.

This point was, I think, for me the climax of feeling in the whole experience; I was incapable of any further sensation – that is any further sensation in the same direction. But here the abominable character of the affair showed itself most plainly, for it suddenly presented an entirely new aspect to me. The light fell on the picture from a new angle, and galvanised me into a fresh ability to feel when I thought a merciful numbness had supervened. It may not sound a great deal in the printed letter, but it came to me almost as if it had been an extension of consciousness, for the Hand that held the pencil suddenly touched in with ghastly effect of contrast the element of the ludicrous. Nothing could have been worse just then. Shorthouse, the masterful spirit, so intrepid in the affairs of ordinary life, whose power increased rather than lessened in the face of danger – this man, creeping on hands and knees along a rafter in a barn at three o'clock in the morning, watching me all the time as a cat watches a mouse! Yes, it was distinctly ludicrous, and while it gave me a measure with which to gauge the dread emotion that caused his aberration, it stirred somewhere deep in my interior the strings of an empty laughter.

One of those moments then came to me that are said to come sometimes under the stress of great emotion, when in an instant the mind grows dazzlingly clear. An abnormal lucidity took the place of my confusion of thought, and I suddenly understood that the two dreams which I had taken for nightmares must really have been sent me, and that I had been allowed for one moment to look over the edge of what was to come; the Good was helping, even when the Evil was most determined to destroy.

I saw it all clearly now. Shorthouse had over-rated his strength. The terror inspired by his first visit to the barn (when he had failed) had roused the man's whole nature to win, and he had brought me to divert the deadly stream of evil. That he had again underrated the power against him was apparent as soon as he entered the barn, and his wild talk, and refusal to admit what he felt, were due to this desire not to acknowledge the insidious fear that was growing in his heart. But, at length, it had become too strong. He had left my side in my sleep –. had been overcome himself, perhaps, first in. *his* sleep, by the dreadful impulse. He knew that I should interfere, and with every movement he made, he watched me steadily, for the mania was upon him and he was *determined to hang himself.* He pretended not to hear me calling, and I knew that anything coming between him and his purpose would meet the full force of his fury – the fury of a maniac, of one, for the time being, truly possessed.

For a minute or two I sat there and stared. I saw then for the first time that there was a bit of rope trailing after him, and that this was what made the rustling sound I had noticed. Shorthouse, too, had come to a stop. His body lay along the rafter like a crouching animal. He was looking hard at me. That whitish patch was his face.

I can lay claim to no courage in the matter, for I must confess that in one sense I was frightened almost beyond control. But at the same time the necessity for decided action, if I was to save his life, came to me with an intense relief. No matter what animated him for the moment, Shorthouse was only a *man*; it was flesh and blood I had to contend with and not the intangible powers. Only a few hours before I had seen him cleaning his gun, smoking his pipe, knocking the billiard balls about with very human clumsiness, and the picture flashed across my mind with the most wholesome effect.

Then I dashed across the floor of the barn and leaped upon the hay bales as a preliminary to climbing up the sides to the first rafter. It was far more difficult than in my dream. Twice I slipped back into the hay, and as I scrambled up for the third time I saw that Shorthouse, who thus far had made no sound or movement, was now busily doing something with his hands upon the beam. He was at its further end, and there must have been fully fifteen feet between us. Yet I saw plainly what he was doing; he was fastening the rope to the rafter. *The other end, I saw, was already round his neck!*

This gave me at once the necessary strength, and in a second I had swung myself on to a beam, crying aloud with all the authority I could put into my voice –

'You fool, man! What in the world are you trying to do? Come down at once!'

My energetic actions and words combined had an immediate effect upon him for which I blessed Heaven; for he looked up from his horrid task, stared hard at me for a second or two, and then came wriggling along like a great cat to intercept me. He came by a series of leaps and bounds and at an astonishing pace, and the way he moved somehow inspired me with a fresh horror, for it did not seem the natural movement of a human being at all, but more, as I have said, like that of some lithe wild animal.

He was close upon me. I had no clear idea of what exactly I meant to do. I could see his face plainly now; he was grinning cruelly; the eyes were positively luminous, and the menacing expression of the mouth was most distressing to look upon. Otherwise it was the face of a chalk man, white and dead, with all the semblance of the living human drawn out of it. Between his teeth he held my clasp knife, which he must have taken from me in my sleep, and with a flash I recalled his anxiety to know which pocket it was in.

'Drop that knife!' I shouted at him, 'and drop after it yourself –'

'Don't you dare to stop me!' he hissed, the breath coming between his lips across the knife that he held in his teeth. 'Nothing in the world can stop me now – I have promised – and I must do it. I can't hold out any longer.'

'Then drop the knife and I'll help you,' I shouted back in his face. 'I promise –'

'No use,' he cried, laughing a little, 'I must do it and you can't stop me.'

I heard a sound of laughter, too, somewhere in the air behind me. The next second Shorthouse came at me with a single bound.

To this day I cannot quite tell how it happened. It is still a wild confusion and a fever of horror in my mind, but from somewhere I drew more than my usual allowance of strength, and before he could well have realised what I meant to do, I had his throat between my fingers. He opened his teeth and the knife dropped at once, for I gave him a squeeze he need never forget. Before, my muscles had felt like so much soaked paper; now they recovered their natural strength, and more besides. I managed to work ourselves along the rafter until the hay was beneath us, and then, completely exhausted, I let go my hold and we swung round together and dropped on to the hay, he clawing at me in the air even as we fell.

The struggle that began by my fighting for his life ended in a wild effort to save my own, for Shorthouse was quite beside himself, and had no idea what he was doing. Indeed, he has always averred that he remembers nothing of the entire night's experiences after the time when he first woke me from sleep. A sort of deadly mist settled over him, he declares, and he lost all sense of his own identity. The rest was a blank until he came to his senses under a mass of hay with me on the top of him.

It was the hay that saved us, first by breaking the fall and then by impeding his movements so that I was able to prevent his choking me to death.